# The Christmas Owl

Fulton Books
Meadville, PA

Published by Fulton Books 2022

ISBN 978-1-63985-444-8 (paperback)
ISBN 978-1-63985-445-5 (digital)

Printed in the United States of America

# The Christmas Owl

Jennifer Schairer

"They're coming! They're coming!" screamed the forest animals. There was a flurry of excitement as they scampered through the fresh, fluffy snow to the center of the grand pine trees. The owl sisters flew down to find out what the excitement was all about.

Hannah, the white snow bunny, squealed, "The humans are coming! It's that time when they choose a grand pine tree to represent Christmas."

Hope, Faith, and Joy were thrilled to hear the news.

"I wonder who they will choose," Hope said with curiosity.

"It is such an honor for a grand pine to be selected," stated Faith.

"I want to learn all about Christmas!" screamed Joy.

The animals carefully tucked themselves away to watch the humans walk the forest and admire the grand pine trees. The pines were at their best that day. Each had fresh snow perfectly placed on several branches, sparkling in the morning sun. After hours of walking and careful discussion, a tree was chosen.

"Oh my!" screamed Joy.

Hope shrieked, "They have chosen Grandpa Pine!"

Faith could not utter a word; she was in shock.

Ben, the local tree farmer, would help take the tree down. Ben and his brother, Christian, would return the next day with their dad, Paul, to remove the majestic grand pine tree.

After the humans left, the animals gathered around the pine tree to say goodbye. It was an exciting time, a privilege, but also sad. They thanked the pine tree for the years of love and friendship. For providing a safe home for them all these wonderful years. The white snow bunny Hannah, along with her brothers and sisters, lived under the tree. It was a great memory she would never forget. The Owl sisters Hope, Faith, and Joy, along with their parents, flew up in the branches and hugged one another as they thanked Grandpa Pine, as the sister called the tree. They had been living within the branches forever and would now need to leave for a new home.

The owl family spent their last night together in the loving branches of Grandpa Pine. They spent the night telling stories and telling Grandpa Pine how proud they were that he was chosen.

But Joy did not understand. She was quite confused, sad, and well, a little bit mad. "What is Grandpa Pine chosen to do?" cried Joy.

Joy's parents explained that each year a beautiful grand pine was chosen to represent Christmas in New York City. People from all over the world would come and admire the grand pine tree. Grandpa would be the Rockefeller Christmas Tree. He would help spread happiness and love to all who believed.

Joy was still very curious, so she stated, "I want to go!" But her parents told her that the chosen tree must make the Christmas journey alone. This did not sit well with Joy.

Early in the morning, as the sun was rising, with golden beams of light glistening on the snow, the animals awoke and gathered in the center of the grand pines. Together, as they finished, the other grand pines formed a circle around the tree and wished him well, telling him once again how much they loved him. After, the other grand pine trees magically bowed their limbs in a loving goodbye to Grandpa Pine.

Soon the sound of the trucks could be heard in the air. The animals vanished out of sight but remained close by to watch Grandpa Pine leave on his Christmas journey.

Ben and Christian, along with their dad, Paul, carefully wrapped Grandpa Pine's branches with netting and tied them firmly to protect each one. With a booming, cracking sound, Grandpa Pine began to shake and rock back and forth. The animals held hands and their breath as they watched from the safety of their shelter. In moments, Grandpa Pine came crashing to the ground, shaking all in the area. The sound was powerful, causing the young animals to hide in their parents' arms. But Joy, she stood alone and watched in both fear and amazement. When Grandpa Pine landed, she was sure he was hurt, but all the others began to cheer, which told her he was fine.

The men carefully loaded Grandpa Pine onto the trailer with a large crane and tied him down for his protection. The animals waved goodbye until Grandpa was almost out of sight. And at that moment, Faith and Hope yelled, "Joy! No! Come back!" They both noticed Joy peeping out of the branches of Grandpa Pine.

It was a long journey to New York City for Grandpa Pine and Joy. Suddenly, Grandpa noticed Joy in his branches. He questioned her, "Joy, why are you here, dear, sweet owlet?"

"I wanted to see what is so special about Christmas and where you are going," Joy said in a nervous little voice.

"Dear Joy, your family will be worried," Grandpa Pine softly whispered to Joy so as not to upset her.

"I'll be okay and will fly home when I learn all about Christmas. I'll travel by night, when my vision is superb," proclaimed Joy.

"Please, Grandpa, I must learn about Christmas!" Joy begged.

"Well, not much we can do about it now, so stay safely tucked in my bottom branches, Joy," ordered Grandpa Pine. Joy did as she was told and soon fell fast asleep, one more time wrapped in Grandpa Pine's warm branches.

After several hours, Joy and Grandpa woke up to a loud noise. Noises they had never heard before. It seemed a busy city had many noises not found in the forest. Suddenly, the truck came to a screeching stop. At that moment, a thunderous sound took over the sky. There were many people standing around, clapping at the arrival of Grandpa Pine. There were smiles on the faces of all, and children jumping about. It was a magnificent sight to see.

Grandpa Pine whispered to Joy, "Remain still and hidden deep within my branches." Joy did just as she was told; she was quite nervous.

A large group of volunteers led by Ben, Christian, and Paul lifted Grandpa Pine with a huge crane. The crane carefully lifted the majestic pine and carried him to the center of Rockefeller Center. Grandpa Pine was placed in a large stand, secured in place. Christian yelled for all to back up. On a count of three, Ben, Paul, and Christian cut the netting away from Grandpa Pine. This allowed his huge branches to drop into place, showing all why he was the chosen tree for this year's celebration. The entire place exploded with roaring applause. Grandpa Pine was a star! His branches dropped perfectly in place, filling the entire area with love, hope, and Christmas joy.

The volunteers got right to work adorning Grandpa with Christmas lights. Thousands of lights illuminated him for all to see day and night. A huge star was lastly placed on top of Grandpa Pine. It was brilliant, golden, and there for all to see. And once again, as if programmed, the entire area erupted into a grand round of applause. Joy had the best view of all, hidden inside Grandpa Pine. She excitedly watched as the volunteers illuminated Grandpa, and jumped when the lights turned on. She watched as the star was lifted up past her branch and carefully placed on top. She looked below as all cheered and clapped for Grandpa Pine.

Then, the most beautiful sound filled the air, and the crowd sang. They sang "Oh, Christmas Tree." This moved Joy to tears. She watched as the people took pictures of Grandpa Pine and as they hugged one another, gazing up at him. She saw a man propose to his girlfriend, and parents hug their children with the deepest, most loving hugs. And she felt Grandpa Pine stand taller and stretch out his branches more and more. He was filled with pride. He was the chosen tree.

The first night, Joy stayed in the safety of Grandpa Pine, or, as the visitors called him, the Rockefeller Christmas Tree. Joy could not believe the line of visitors that came from all directions to see the beauty that was Grandpa Pine.

At this moment, Joy was not very careful, and a volunteer fixing one of the lights on Grandpa was suddenly nose to beak with Joy. The volunteer, Mr. Stan, removed his plaid scarf from around his neck and carefully gathered up Joy within it. He was so gentle that Joy was not afraid. Grandpa whispered, "Love you, Joy! You will be safe with Mr. Stan. Tell all back home I made it and that I love them too." Joy was carefully carried and brought down in the buck lift with Mr. Stan.

The discovery of Joy was just as exciting as the lighting of Grandpa Pine. Except the crowd hushed, and all stared lovingly at Joy. A small little girl, named Olivia, proclaimed, "A Christmas owl." The entire group was overjoyed and clapped. Children climbed on top of their parents' shoulders to get a glimpse of the Christmas owl.

Mr. Stan carefully walked Joy through the crowd as all exploded with love for the Christmas owl. Joy was carefully taken to Mr. Stan's wife, Dot, to be cared for until they could drive Joy back to her home. Ms. Dot placed Joy in a warm cage, with food and water. Wrapped in Mr. Stan's plaid scarf. She watched over Joy all night. The next day, arrangements were made to take Joy back to the forest, where she would be safe and sound.

Ms. Dot had her television on, and she noticed that reporters were standing next to the Rockefeller Christmas Tree, reporting on the love all not only had for Grandpa Pine but also for the Christmas owl they had nicknamed Rocky. Children brought pictures they drew of the owlet and hung each on the branches of Grandpa Pine. The arrival of Joy brought thousands more to see the Christmas pair, Grandpa Pine and Joy. There was an extra layer of love, love because Joy was there. The crowd called their little visitor a miracle and fell in love with the owlet.

Mr. Stan and Ms. Dot brought Joy to Rockefeller Center before leaving for her home in the forest. The crowd was happy to get another look at the Christmas owl. The little owl that filled everyone's heart. The discovery of Joy gave all a renewed feeling of love, of Christmas spirit.

Joy returned home safely wrapped in a warm blanket on Ms. Dot's lap while Mr. Stan drove. They listened to the radio play Christmas songs and spoke of the beautiful tree and the adorable owlet who came to Rockefeller Center. Joy brought so much happiness and extra Christmas joy to all.

20

Joy's sisters, Hope and Faith, squealed with excitement when they saw Joy. Hannah, the white snow bunny, Joy's best friend, hopped over to welcome her home. Joy's parents flew down from the trees wanting to reprimand her but could only hug her tightly. Joy told them all of the adventure and how proud Grandpa Pine stood and the love he brought to all. The renewed faith that grew in each and every person who gazed lovingly at him. She shared how she was discovered and how she was loved and accepted by all as the Christmas owl, Rocky.

Joy found the meaning of Christmas; it was the feeling of love, hope, and faith in all. She was happy to have shared the moment with Grandpa Pine and her family.

The following year, Joy and her sisters, Hope and Faith, flew day and night to Rockefeller Center to see the new Christmas tree. To their surprise, a small owl ornament was placed on the tree. People not only came to admire the tree but also took photos of the little owl, "Rocky," on the tree. They had not forgotten the special little owl that filled their hearts with Christmas joy. The sisters were crying happy tears as they gazed at the crowd with the owl ornament.

The little curious owl lived up to her name and brought more Christmas joy than anyone could ever imagine.

# About the Author

Born in Somers Point, New Jersey, and spending her childhood on the beach and boardwalk of Ocean City is our author, Jennifer Schairer. She is married to her husband, Paul, and they have three children: Hannah, Ben, and Christian.

Jennifer has been an elementary school teacher in Mays Landing, New Jersey, since 1992. She loves to be with her family, especially her parents, Dot and Stan, as well as her sisters, cousins, and friends she considers her family. Jennifer enjoys crafting, shopping, walking, going to the beach, entertaining all year round, decorating for the holidays, and especially loves floating in the pool with a great book to read.